goodbye earth
hello moon

¡Que te vaya bien!

Printed in the United States on recycled paper made up of 30% post-consumer waste.

www.warren-machine.com

for our families

A deep blue sky
And soft white snow
Touched the leaves of the trees
On the planet we know.

Cities and newspapers,
Cars, bars and parks,
Freeways and skyscrapers
Glowed in the dark.

Giraffes with long necks roamed thick grassy lands.
Turtles were quiet and lay in the sand.

There were monkeys in trees,
Bears sleeping on mountains,

Penguins on ice,
Whales spitting up fountains.

Days came and went,
good times were had.
Frogs sang their songs
and foxes were bad.

One day round the table and a glass of ice water,
The penguins declared, "You know, it got a lot hotter!"

Let's have an adventure!
And go somewhere new!
We'll call all our friends,
so they can come too!

"Hasta luego, Tierra del Fuego!"

"Au revoir, Zanzibar"

"Have sweet dreams, Rivers and Streams!"

"See you later, dear Equator!"

"Cheerio, Mountains and Snow!"

"Sayonara, great Sahara!"

"Ciao ciao, Palau"

So off they floated
up into the sky,
with just enough time
for one last goodbye.

The turtles and tigers,
birds and baboons,
said, "Goodbye Earth,"